# T W I N S

## A Coming-of-Age Novella

by

Laura Krieger Emack

# Dedication

This volume is dedicated to Tori's Nana, my best friend BettiAnn O'Connell.

Her memory *is* a blessing.

Prospect Press

334 Blanket Lane

Prospect, ME 04981

(207) 567-3437

LKECPA@fairpoint.net

ISBN: 979-8-9953503-0-9

# Spring Time

2012

# CHAPTER 1

Katie adored her grandmother. Every day began the very same way.

"Hi, Nana."

Bright sunlight cut a slatted pattern across the posters on Katie's bedroom wall. There was one from every musical she'd ever been in. Unfortunately, her name never appeared in bold letters. For Katie Monahan was no diva. She carried a tune well, her tone sweet and appealing. But, as the drama coach said after each awful audition, "Katie, you fail to project." Katie sighed. It was her own stupid fault. Try as she might, she couldn't sing loud.

Nana snorted. "Idiot never heard of a microphone?"

If only Nana had been there! She would have interfered; she would have forcibly argued Katie's case. Come to think of it - and Katie had been doing a whole lot of thinking lately - it wasn't one bit fair. How could the stupid school continue to pick the same popular girls for starring roles every single year?

"What about Alice?" demanded Nana. "Where the hell was Alice when they picked the leading lady?"

Katie knew that answer. Mom was working.

Oh, how Katie longed to be glam and gorgeous! She had an okay face that stayed, thank God, zit-free. Everyone said she was pretty, but people said all kinds of stuff without meaning it, and Katie often doubted their sincerity. No, Katie feared she would always get lost in the crowd. Now, it was absolutely true that she danced well. Her final score in life, plusses and minuses, added up to Katie Monahan landing in the chorus every time. At least she usually got to stand in the front row.

Soon, very soon, high school would be freaking history. No more math homework! No more jocks blocking the hallway in front of her locker. No more getting up at the crack of dawn to catch the stupid school bus. The popular kids, like Bethany and Gina, all drove to school. It sucked having to ride the cheese wagon like a little kid. It sucked living in a rented duplex with Mom.

Then she remembered what day it was. Katie grinned at Nana. Unsure if her grandmother had access to such details, she said, "Guess what, Nana. This is a special day."

"Why's that?" asked Nana.

"First of all, there's no school today."

The happy details came rushing back. Because there was no school, Mom had said yes, Katie could work until closing time the night before. She'd fallen into bed, exhausted after waitressing extra-long at the Olive Garden. She had forgotten to twist the wand on the window shade closed. Now as she sat up in bed, sun-and-shade bars locked Chad Kimball and Betsy Gibrone, a/k/a Tony and Maria, in jail. It served them right for being chosen.

She extracted her feet from the tangled sheets. She still wore the frumpy pantyhose her boss insisted they all wear at work. Talk about lame! Practically nobody sold plain pantyhose anymore. The boutiques where Bethany shopped sold colorful leggings and blingy tights that went perfectly with miniskirts. The old pantyhose from Mom's dresser drawer had a hideous control top designed to squish fat.

Katie's slender curves needed no help from spandex. Her face might be ho-hum, but her skin was spotless. She didn't have a single birthmark. She only had one little scar behind her left knee. She never had gotten any tattoos, as Nana disliked them on girls. Not to mention it hurt like hell getting one. No, Katie had nothing whatsoever to hide.

Katie's stomach lurched. But did she have enough to show?

"Are you sure about tonight, Honey?" Nana asked with deep concern.

"We've been through all that," Katie countered with steely near-certitude.

"I'm just asking."

Katie stepped into the hallway and opened the door to the bathroom. She peeled off the nasty pantyhose. She dropped them on top of her crumpled white uniform in the hamper. Then she took the T shirt off. Nana always wore a T shirt to bed back when Katie used to stay at her place overnight.

Katie spotted her cell phone on the vanity. It said 9:45. Perfect! Mom would have showered and left for work ages ago. Mrs. Gormley, their landlady who lived on the other side of the duplex, was away in Boston. So, there would be rivers of hot water and nobody to bug Katie for using up every last trickle.

Katie stood under the pelting spray, thinking how much high school sucked. She was damn sick of doing ridiculously hard things, like quadratic equations, for no reward in the short or long term. Working could suck too, but she got a check every week from the Olive Garden, plus cash tips.

Last fall, she had nearly failed trigonometry, getting by with the one and only D on her report card. Katie finally stood mere weeks away from graduating. Then what? Mom wanted her to go to college. She'd been accepted at U Maine. No place else.

"Not now," injected Nana with infinite wisdom. "Enjoy this moment."

Nana was right. Katie had the house to herself. Today was about looking good, really good. Bigger than that. She needed to look perfectly wonderful! Katie carefully applied cream rinse to her long hair.

Bare naked, Katie opened the hallway door to clear the steam from the shower. She scampered to fetch the Rite-Aid bag from her purse in the bedroom. She bent over the hand mirror.

Katie happily chatted with Nana as she tried out the new, sparkly, silver eye shadow.

"I didn't use up the hot water. Not quite anyway. So I'm not a spoiled brat. Am I, Nana?"

Senior year would be over in six weeks. Senior year was a freaking joke. Still, they made them go through the motions day after day. But not today.

"I love teacher training days. Don't you, Nana?"

"They need it. That's for sure."

Katie giggled. Nana didn't pretend respect for all grownups like most other adults.

"This is the best Friday of all. At least till graduation."

"You're not a child anymore, Katie."

It was literally true. She was just barely of legal age. All around her, classmates kept turning eighteen. Her time finally came, but not until late March. There had been no birthday party because she never invited people home. Christ, if you turned your freaking stereo up one single notch, Mrs. Gormley came pounding on the front door. Someday Katie would live in a big house with a deck and a yard and no asshole landlady.

Mom's job since forever was at the phone company. As a supervisor, she dressed in mannish suits. Katie knew that Mom always wore a Spanx underneath because, let's face it, Mom needed major help squashing her fat. Mom blamed motherhood and her desk job instead of admitting she'd let herself go (which Katie vowed to never ever do). Mom was forever telling people how many hours of overtime she had to work to become a supervisor at the age of thirty-seven. Like it was a big deal bossing around a bunch of dumb phone operators.

"I mean, who brags about working for the freaking phone company?" asked Katie. "You know what I mean, Nana. It's okay for some people, but not for you and me."

Katie wasn't exactly sure what Nana used to do for work. She always had twenty-dollar bills in her purse, though, and loved to spend them on treats for Katie.

What path in life would suit Katie just right? The sixty-four-gazillion-dollar question loomed. Soon, very soon, she would have to provide an official written answer for the graduation program. Entering the workforce, the default answer for losers, simply would not do.

"I don't know. I don't know," she muttered. "Come on, Nana. What do you think?"

Katie paused, closed her eyes, and listened real hard. Sometimes an answer came that way. She stood, purple eyeliner poised. Nana said nothing at all.

"Tell me what to do!" she screeched.

Suddenly, a shadow lurked. "Who the hell are you talking to?" Mom's voice sounded extra ugly.

Katie jumped, drawing an errant violet streak on her cheek. Thinking fast, Katie lied and said she was rehearsing for an audition. It was a pretty convincing lie, as they were casting for the last musical of her school career. She rarely auditioned anymore, but she might have changed her mind.

Well, it would have been a convincing lie except that Mom asked which role and what play. And instead of just spitting out "Shirley" or "Marlena" and any old made-up play title, Katie hesitated.

Mom figured it out fast. It wasn't like she didn't already know that Katie kept talking to Nana long after the funeral. But as she approached adolescence, Katie understood that she must keep those conversations with her grandmother super secret. As a result, she had not been caught in the act for a very long time.

"It's been nine years, Katie. Nine years since my mother died!"

Mom went on a veritable tirade, calling Katie a baby and accusing her of making Nana over into some kind of saint the woman never was. It was an ancient script, an old argument. Mom knew where the buttons were.

"Know what? Next time I see her, I'm going to tell Bethany that you have an imaginary friend."

"You wouldn't!"

Katie felt deeply stung. She willed away tears that started spilling anyway.

"Oh, fuck her!" whispered Nana in Katie's inner ear.

Katie suddenly giggled.

That made Mom extremely mad, pissed enough to say the F word herself, which she never, ever did.

"What's so fucking funny?"

"Nothing."

Katie's denial was automatic. Then she had an inspiration. She knew where certain buttons were located too.

"What are you doing at home on a weekday anyway? Did you lose your job?"

Mom blanched. "What a terrible thing to say!"

"Well done," whispered Nana. "Major ouch."

Katie giggled again.

"For your information, young lady, I am in no danger whatsoever of losing my position," countered Mom, her voice a mix of fury and veiled, visceral panic.

"Okay, okay. Calm down," said Katie.

"It so happens that they shut the power off on our entire floor to rewire the network today. That's why I'm home from work on a weekday."

"Oh." Katie's heart sank. "So you've got the day off?"

"Unfortunately, just the morning." It was Mom's turn to sling another barb. "I'm surprised you're out of bed before noon."

In Katie's inner ear, Nana pointed out how Mom never missed an opportunity to pick on poor Katie. It was true, but Katie didn't feel like wasting time squabbling. It could still be a good day. She meant to have an awesome afternoon and a magical evening. She'd settle for several hours alone to rehearse, to experiment with her hair, and to borrow the pair of silver high-heeled shoes in Mom's closet.

Katie decided to play the gracious card for a change. "At least you get the morning off. They're paying you for the time, right?"

"Damn right they are."

Mom actually smiled, making her look younger. She didn't look youthful, but she certainly looked better than usual. In a cheery Mommy voice, she asked, "So what are you up to today, Sweetie?"

"Nothing much," answered Katie.

"Are you working again tonight?"

"Uh huh."

To herself she added the words, "but not where you think."

"That's nice. I hope the tips are good."

Katie decided not to continue the conversation. So far she hadn't actually lied about her plans. With luck, Mom would wander off to do her own thing, whatever that might be, if Katie ignored her.

Katie bent toward the mirror to apply strawberry lip gloss. Would there be tips tonight? She wasn't quite sure what to expect in that regard. If not, she would happily walk away with the two crisp one-hundred-dollar bills that had been promised to her. Katie loved tips. Men tipped better than women, especially when she flirted with them just a little bit.

Mom spoke again. 'Don't forget to make your bed. And that bathroom hamper is full to the brim."

"So?"

That was stupid of her. Katie knew the answer, which came with speed and vigor.

"So run a goddamn load of laundry. Take out the stuff that's in the dryer, fold it properly, and put it away in the drawers this time. I'm not your slave."

It took all her strength not to snap back, but Katie held her tongue. If she said something sassy, there'd be more chores added to the list, and the whole afternoon would get wasted. She'd spend all her free time doing what some bossy grownup told her to do.

Katie reached for the blow dryer and turned it on.

Mom emitted a put-upon sigh. "Well, I hope you didn't use every drop of hot water."

Finally, finally, finally, Mom left the bathroom.

Katie detested her mother. "I just hate her, don't you?" She hissed the question, careful not to be overheard talking to Nana again.

Hate Alice?

Like God, Nana declined to answer.

## CHAPTER 2

The night before his birthday, Ralph decided not to set the alarm. He clicked off the TV with David Letterman yet to reveal the day's top-ten list. Sometimes the payoff was worth it, sometimes not so much. Sleep came quickly in the big bed. It was easier to sleep alone than with Sherry, his ex-wife, who loved to prattle on about nothing.

A mere five hours later, his eyes popped open. Damn! His soul was programmed. Ralph had no appointments to keep, as he had cleared the day's calendar. There was no dog to let out, no sons to wake up in time to catch the school bus. Those days were long gone.

The new woodstove downstairs wouldn't need reloading for several hours. Still, he awoke at dawn just like any old day. It was pointless to fight the urge to piss.

Ralph stood undeniably wide awake, bare feet on cold tile. So much for sleeping in on his birthday. Number sixty. The figure felt incomprehensible.

"Un-fucking believable," muttered Ralph as he descended the stairs. Not one damn muscle hurt, though, he noted with pride. His dick still worked too, not that it got much action these days. This was by choice, a temporary hiatus sliding toward habit.

Ralph entered the kitchen and flipped on the coffee maker that he'd set up the night before. This was among the small tasks painlessly absorbed into his routine since Sherry's second departure two years earlier. He stood and looked around while the machine burped and sputtered.

His kitchen boasted the best of old and new. The ceiling was real plaster, expertly applied by a guy who didn't charge too much. The wainscoting was original, and the chair rail too. The floor looked like hardwood but was actually Pergo. The modern product was hard to damage and easy to maintain. Granite countertops gleamed all about.

Ruefully, Ralph admitted to himself that he enjoyed polishing the flecked black stone to a perfect sheen. Ralph kept the place plenty clean enough. Sherry had been a manic housecleaner, picking up after them in intrusive ways that made clear their male ineptitude. He'd surprised himself after the final rupture. Funny the way you bought somebody else's narrative about yourself. He was not, in fact, a slob.

After all, Ralph had been cleaning up old houses for years, actually for several decades. Major messes left behind by dead homeowners or sketchy tenants, that was part and parcel of buying and restoring wrecks with good bones. After the junkman left with the last truckload, he would inspect every inch while vacuuming corners and hand-wiping woodwork. Picking up after one grown man? Not a problem.

Only one thing jarred Ralph's sense of style as he slouched against the kitchen island. A kitschy, flowered stencil ringed the room overhead. It contained well-worn sayings, women's wisdom, repeated ad nauseum. *Home is where the heart is. It is better to give than to receive. Love conquers all.* Hah! The hell it did. Death conquers all was more like it.

Ralph mentally kicked himself. How had he ever let Sherry talk him into putting up that tasteless stencil? With his own hands, no less. When Sherry took off the first time, Ralph immediately replaced the red-heart knobs that Sherry had chosen for the cabinets with cut glass ones salvaged from a demolition site. How could he have missed this greatest offense of all? That shit had to go and fast! Maybe even today. No, not today because today was his birthday.

And it was, indeed, a beautiful spring day beyond the bay window. Green maple seeds littered the backyard, covering it almost as completely as the red leaves of autumn. The maples were always the first to turn color in September. He was deep in thought over a second cup of coffee when the phone rang.

He checked the caller ID before picking up. Shit! The caller was Sherry. It bugged him mightily that she knew he'd be up at the crack of dawn, even on his birthday although Ralph was his own boss. It bugged him even more that she was right. He let the call go to voicemail. He listened.

Then he exploded. "Fuck no!"

Sherry was planning to come over to make him a birthday dinner in the kitchen she knew so well. Ralph picked up the receiver.

"Hi, Sherry."

It took her a second to grasp that he'd interrupted her breathless onslaught of words.

"Don't," he said. "I mean it. Just don't."

"Why not?"

Sherry's distress was so keen, the hurt so palpable, that something in Ralph cracked. The edge of the ice floe melted. Sure, she'd been the one who left him way back when. She ran off with some flaming asshole she met on the internet. Genuine regret had followed quickly on Sherry's part, but Ralph did not take her back. Not right away, that is.

Sherry used to set up the coffee. Sherry used to scrub the floors, to make out the Christmas cards in both their names. Had and would again if he was dumb enough to let her move back into his house, into his world. The slide felt comfortable and familiar. She would fuck his brains out tonight. Suck his cock too. Oh, that slide.

"It's not a good idea," Ralph muttered weakly.

"You know," offered Sherry. "They say the third time is the charm."

That did it! Leave it to Sherry to push too hard, to make it abundantly clear that one birthday dinner would lead straight to everything. By now he knew the pattern. There would be abundant, extravagant sex for a while. Then the nagging would start. Sex would become a scarce commodity, a reward to be earned. It wasn't just the nagging. Far worse was the endless, pointless chatter. God, the woman never shut up!

"Ralph. Are you there?" Sherry's high-pitched voice, never a selling point, sounded mighty shaky.

"Look, Sherry," he said. Relief poured into him, warm like the perfect coffee in his cup. Sherry never made it quite strong enough. Yes, he had a way out of this morass, one that need not inflict more pain upon the mother of his children. "I appreciate the gesture, Sherry. Really, I do. But the boys are planning a birthday bash."

"They are? What kind of bash? You don't suppose I could -"

"No," he interrupted firmly. "I don't suppose you can come."

"Why not?"

"Because it's Carl and Jim's ballgame. That's why."

"All the more reason."

It was so predictable, Sherry playing the family card. Not this time. What was the saying? Fool me once, shame on you. Fool me twice, shame on me. Fool me three times? That was not about to happen. There would be no capitulation, no surrender of his autonomy. Sherry persisted, but Ralph stood firm. What he told her next was the absolute truth.

"I have no idea what the boys have planned."

"I believe you, okay? You don't know. But I bet you could find out. Jim never could keep a secret. Why don't you call him?"

"Nope! It's completely out of my hands. But hey, Sherry. Thanks for remembering my birthday."

It felt cruel, but he hung up at the end of the sentence as if he were dismissing a telemarketer. Hey, it was his damn birthday. Surely, he had the right to decide what went down on this particular day.

No, he did not know what his two sons had in mind. They meant to show him a good time. He was genuinely touched by their shared excitement and their desire to please him. After all, it wasn't every day that Carl and Jim cooperated on anything.

Ralph reveled in the silence of solitude. Some birds began to chirp as the sun rose over the horizon. He recognized the *cheerio* of robins returned from their southerly migration. They said that spring brought hope and renewal, but what did renewal mean to a man turning sixty?

He decided to tackle the back lawn, knowing that a sense of accomplishment - small but pleasurable - would come with the steady revelation of emergent green grass under the thick layer of maple seeds. It wasn't brilliant, but it was a viable plan for the morning.

As to the birthday party come evening? Whatever was set to transpire, Ralph felt damn sure it contemplated no wives and surely no ex-wives.

## CHAPTER 3

Katie shivered in her thin sleeveless dress while Bethany rang the doorbell. The little brick house stood on a tree-lined street in an unfamiliar Bangor neighborhood. It had a little, square, front yard, as did all the nearby places. It wasn't a fancy part of town, but any single-family house surpassed a rented half a home.

"Just a minute," some guy called from within.

"That would be Jim," instructed Bethany. "This is his place."

"Is he the birthday boy?"

Bethany's voice suddenly got throaty. "You wish. Jim's hot. His older brother Carl is too. I'd fuck them both for nothing."

Katie was shocked. She tried to hide her naiveté, but it was too late.

"The look on your face, Katie! It's too much." Bethany was laughing like crazy.

They heard approaching footsteps.

Bethany turned serious. "Be nice to the brothers. They're paying the bill."

Katie swallowed. She thought of a fortyish man in a plaid shirt and baseball cap who always sat in her section at the Olive Garden. Kissing him wasn't totally unthinkable.

"I'll be nice to father and sons," she asserted with breezy confidence.

The hallway introductions were brief. Jim led them into the living room.

"Awesome place!" Katie said. That seemed like a nice thing to offer as an ice breaker. She discovered the compliment to be true, as she looked around at the renovated, semi-open downstairs.

It was the other brother Carl, who sat cracking his knuckles on the couch, who answered. "Dad bought it for next to nothing. It's what we all do for a living."

Carl was stockier than Jim with lines about his mouth, but otherwise the brothers looked alike. They had curly black hair and muscular forearms and boot-clad feet. Big boot-clad feet. Katie smiled to herself; for she knew what they said about men with big feet.

"Want a beer? Jim queried.

Bethany declined, so Katie did too.

"Well. You boys want to check out the goods now?" asked Bethany.

"Absolutely," said Carl

"Can't wait," added Jim.

Suddenly, everybody was looking right at Katie.

"Can't wait for what?" she asked, puzzled.

Carl let out a nasty snicker. "To see the fucking goods."

"Go ahead," said Bethany.

Katie turned toward the cool, popular girl who was not really her friend.

"Jesus, Katie! Take your damn dress off," ordered Bethany.

"Oh."

Katie felt herself blush. As instructed by Bethany for the occasion, she had donned not a stitch of underwear beneath the silver sheath. Six eyes bored into her, Bethany's the brightest and most eager of all. So that's what it felt like to be a star. Bizarrely, she thought of Nana. Long-legged, blond Nana. Suddenly Nana stood smiling in the far corner of the room, encouraging Katie to be brave.

"Okay," said Katie aloud to the room. "Sure thing."

She wasn't wearing Mom's silver stiletto heels, not yet. (Why Mom bought such things when she hadn't had a date in decades, Katie had no idea. Hope must truly spring eternal.) The awesome silver shoes were out in Bethany's car. At the moment Katie had polka-dot Crocs on sockless feet, like some little kid.

Nonetheless, Katie stepped into the center of the room, faced Carl on the couch, and smiled. She'd spent enough time onstage to know the value of the dramatic pause.

You could have heard a pin drop.

A car door slammed somewhere nearby.

With both hands, Katie hooked the hem of her knee-length dress with her fingertips. She was glad she'd taken the time to paint her nails lavender. She raised the dress slowly up her thighs. She felt the brush of her pubic hair against the silken fabric. Again she paused. She took a breath.

A thrill rocketed through her being as she lifted the dress past her navel, knowing that her shapely hips narrowed to a fearsome waist. (Somewhere, in some class, some creepy male teacher had once said that's how cavemen chose their mates, by the ratio of their hips to their waist.)

"All natural bush. Yessuh!" said Carl.

"Just like we requested," affirmed Jim.

Katie's nipples stiffened. Sure, they'd reacted before in response to a boy's kiss or caress, to the press of her own fingertips before the bathroom mirror. This time, though, the stimulation was all mental, born of the erotic energy permeating the room, more powerful than mere human touch.

Jim stood tall in the doorway. Carl leaned forward on the couch. Bethany's hand went to her throat. Suddenly,

Katie felt left out. She too wanted to see her magic nipples revealed. Was there a mirror? She caught her partial reflection in one of the long windows on the far wall. Unfortunately, her torso was obscured by a bird feeder on a post, visible in the yard. The feeder was empty of birds, empty of seed.

Wait a minute! Katie suddenly remembered the purpose of the evening, the two hundred dollars that would be hers in a few short hours. *Show them the rest of the goods*, she ordered herself. *This performance is not for you.*

She turned from the window and made eye contact again with Carl. Feeling as powerful as Lady Gaga, Katie lifted her dress above the swell of her breasts. What a rush!

"Holy shit," said the boys in unison.

"You put blush on those girls," announced Bethany. "Sweet."

Katie shook her head. She'd never even thought of such a thing.

"Turn around," said Bethany. "Let them see your ass."

Katie obeyed, making eye contact with Jim in passing.

"Look, boys. No tattoos anywhere. She's perfectly innocent," Bethany decreed with a proprietary sweep of the arm.

Carl let out a wolf whistle. "Ain't she something?"'

"Just what the doctor ordered," said Jim.

Katie raised her arms to remove the dress entirely. She could not wait to twirl naked and drive those two thirty-ish men the rest of the way insane. She'd knock Jim and Carl out of their gourds, and Bethany too. Suddenly Katie became the sexiest being on the whole planet. She was positively born to prance nude in polka-dot Crocs.

"Lucky Dad!" said Carl.

*Dad? Shit!* That was right. The birthday boy was an old fart. She'd have to grit her teeth, damn it, to earn those two hundred dollars. (Maybe more, Bethany had hinted, if the client was especially satisfied.) Oh well, there was always a catch. Besides, that part would take place later. Meantime, for once in her life, Katie Monhan was the absolute center of attention.

Katie lifted her arms. One more second, and she'd be dancing naked and free.

Adored. Worshipped. Desired.

A door creaked. "What's that?" asked Jim.

"Hello?" called a woman's voice from the hallway.

"Oh God, it's Mom," said Jim with a gasp.

"What the fuck!' contributed Carl.

"Your mother is here?" The panic in Bethany's voice was unmistakable. "We've got to get out of here. Now!"

"No shit," Carl answered. He stood and took charge. "Jim. Go deal with Mom. Get her into the kitchen. Okay?"

After a last leer at Katie, who stood with her dress bunched about her neck, Jim left the room. Carl opened one of the big windows and pushed out the screen.

"Sorry about the bum's rush. Bum – ha ha, that's funny."

"Never mind!" said Bethany. "Hurry up."

"Come on," Bethany hissed as she went through the open window into the yard.

Katie lowered her dress and clambered after Bethany. Somebody lifted her dress up again from behind. She felt Carl's hot hands grip her bare buttocks and push firmly. The window closed behind her.

"Good job, Kid," whispered Bethany.

"Thanks," said Katie.

"You're welcome."

Katie laughed out loud at the silly politeness, under the circumstances.

"Shut up!" warned Bethany.

They skirted the property line on their way to Bethany's parked car where the other cheerleaders waited.

"What was so funny back there?"

“Nothing,” answered Katie, realizing she’d just used the same, standard non-answer normally directed at Mom.

“Where the fuck are my keys?”

Katie waited patiently while Bethany fumbled in her purse and swore some more.

“Katie, Katie, Katie,” said a bemused voice in Katie’s head.

“What, Nana?”

“You are a naughty girl.”

“I know. Are you mad at me, Nana?”

“Do I sound mad?”

No, Nana didn’t sound mad. She didn’t sound angry at all. She kind of sounded proud. Impressed anyway.

“You know what, Nana? That was easy. I thought it might be hard, but it was really easy.”

“Life is like that sometimes,” declared Nana wisely.

Bethany finally found her keys.

Katie adjusted her dress as she maneuvered into the cramped middle seat between Tanya and Laurel. They all waited for the brothers to emerge from the house so that the girls could follow the boys to Clyde Somebody’s farm out in the middle of nowhere. Eventually, Carl climbed into the driver’s side of a shiny, four-wheel-drive truck parked in the driveway, and Jim took the passenger side.

She could still feel Carl's leathery hands pushing on her bare behind. She'd always heard that boys liked to look at girls' asses. But she had never once imagined that she could feel such intense sensation there. Of all places.

Carl's hands. Her ass cheeks. How could that simple combination possibly be such a turn on?

Gina, who sat beside Bethany in the front seat, turned around to look at Katie. Gina was the nicest of the four cheerleaders in the car.

"Hey Katie. You still game?"

"Sure thing, Gina. Piece of cake."

## CHAPTER 4

The backyard looked much better when he was done raking. Ralph heard the house phone ring, and he rushed inside to answer it. An unknown number appeared on the caller-ID screen. Not Sherry again. Good. He picked up and said hello. The demonic shriek of a fax transmission blared into his ear.

"Fuck you!" he screamed into the phone. Trouble was, there was no asshole on the other end to hear him protest. Ralph angrily slammed the phone receiver onto its cradle. Something fell off the bulletin board that hung on the kitchen wall.

He bent and picked up the piece of paper. *Roses are red and violets are blue,* stared Ralph in the face as he stood back up. *And shit is brown*, he added mentally.

Yes, that wall border had to go! The vibrant colors would be hard to efface. Too bad he couldn't ask Jim, whose workmanship was careful, to erase his own mother's signature. Ditto for delegating to Carl minus the attention to detail. No, he'd have to do this painstaking remediation himself.

The grandfather clock in the front hall chimed three times. There was still a gap of time to fill before he was to meet up with Carl and Jim at Clyde Barnett's farm. From there, God only knew what the boys had in mind. Meanwhile, the waning afternoon hours of Ralph's sixtieth birthday stretched ahead, unclaimed.

Was he hungry after the hours spent working in the yard? Quite hungry. Eating was predictably pleasurable. Indulging in a double quarter pounder with supersized fries was surely allowable on his birthday. He reached for his keys on the wall hook.

But he stopped short. No, the party later on would feature all kinds of fattening food. There would be hard liquor and a keg or two. Probably a birthday cake. Maybe some hot young slut would even jump out of it. Probably not. Ralph was careful about his weight, proud that he sported no beer belly.

He opened the fridge and sniffed the carton of two-percent milk – it was still good. He added some milk to a bowl of cornflakes. Standing at the counter, he scarfed down the cereal before it could all turn soggy. Some birthday meal. Talk about pathetic!

Ralph glanced at the piece of paper before re-affixing it to the bulletin board. It was an ad that he had clipped from the Bangor Daily News. It described a piece of property on Sebec Lake with a burnt-out cabin. In fact, he knew the place. It was for sale once again. The remains of the cabin needed to be removed, but two acres of mature, mixed timber with lake frontage sounded appealing indeed.

What if he did not limit his thoughts to the realistic, to the possible? What if he could just snap his fingers and say, "Beam me up, Scottie, to Jupiter?" What if he could have his pick of seventy-two gorgeous virgins without, of course, having to blow himself to Kingdom Come for the sake of Allah first?

*Kingdom come all over the place.*

Ralph laughed aloud. It was a stupid pun, but it got his brain unstuck. What else did he crave other than a greasy Macdonald's meal deal or getting laid? Without paying for the latter, of course. Without settling for Sherry either.

Did he long for fame and glory? Not really. He didn't even need the fifteen minutes of fame that were, supposedly, his human due. Better looks? Well, he could stand to be taller than five foot ten. He could definitely stand to be younger. A lot younger than fucking sixty. Beyond that, he couldn't complain about either his God-given face or his build.

Trouble was, back when it might have mattered, back when Ralph should have been free as a bird, his bachelor days were suddenly cut short. His stud days ended before they ever really began.

Nope! Freedom ended when he said "I do" to Sherry, who had skillfully staked her claim while claiming to be on the pill. She sealed it with a little blue circle that signified yes. Yes, the pregnancy test was positive. Yes, there would be baby Carl, moody from the get-go, whose childhood would later be scarred by his parents' bitter separation and divorce.

Oh man, if he could only go back and do it over. Forty years. Thirty years. Ten even. Oh, if he could go back ten years and be with Kristen! With stunning clarity Ralph knew where he wanted to be on the afternoon of his sixtieth birthday.

Sadly, his choice did not lie on the possible side of the spectrum. He decided to go there anyway, alone, to the property with the cabin on Sebec Lake. Clyde Barnett's farm was situated in Piscataquis County too, and that sealed the plan. He could check out the property, then swing over to the farm for his upcoming birthday party.

Ralph stood, threw on his leather jacket, and grabbed his key ring. He would take the old black pickup, a nod to nostalgia that he hoped would not leave him stranded on the side of the road.

The Chevy started hard. Rust had begun to invade the underbody. Ralph took excellent care of his vehicles. But no matter how many times you undercoated a working truck, the body would start to rot long before the mechanics gave out. Ralph hoped the old truck would pass one more state inspection.

A cassette stuck halfway out of the player. Without checking the label, he pressed it into the slot. He liked the uncertainty of not knowing what sound would come next.

At first there was nothing but the annoying whirr of outdated technology. Then *Tangled Up in Blue* began. Ralph remembered that it was one of Kristen's favorites. Riding in the truck together, he and she'd had many insult-laden spats over what constituted enduring music and what was nothing but trendy crap. Bob Dylan's gritty poetics had always spoken to both of them.

Ralph turned off Broadway toward Capehart, chiding himself for the silly detour. He never went there anymore! The cinderblock buildings had changed very little in ten years. To the best of his knowledge, nobody had ever rehabbed the drab units since they once served as military housing back in the sixties. Back when Bangor had an air force base and Miller's famous all-you-can-eat buffet, back when Maine had shoe factories and stud mills.

He pulled to the curb in front of Kristen's old place. No doubt the red tricycle that lay overturned in the driveway of 48 Moosehead Drive belonged to somebody else's grandchild. What was he doing here?

He thought about turning around and heading back home. He even briefly considered calling Sherry and taking her for a ride instead. After all, Sherry was a breathing human being with a warm, wet cunt.

Ralph's right cheek burned; he could have sworn somebody slapped it. Hard! Damn hard! How could he ever confound Kristin's joy and ebullience with Sherry's mindless chatter? Grief, that's how. Ralph swallowed and fought off the sudden need to cry.

Feeling damn stupid, he pretended to honk the horn. He closed his eyes and waited for his girlfriend to arrive. He felt the rush of cold air as the passenger door opened and then closed. He smelled Kristen's scent, a mixture of citrus cologne and high-grade marijuana. She put her hand on his thigh.

"Tell me, Ralph." There was laughter in the lilt of Kristin's imagined voice. "What do you want with a herd of virgins?"

Kristen always had an uncanny ability to read his mind.

"I dunno," he muttered, feeling both cheeks go red-hot.

"Virgins don't have a clue."

"About what?" he teased.

"Like you don't know," she accused.

He adored their banter! He missed the way she challenged him and knocked him off balance. He felt the ancient yearning, the magic anticipation. They were heading to a rustic log cabin with a hundred feet of frontage on Sebec Lake. Powerful desire coursed through them, between them.

This time around he knew that the trip would culminate in the best sex ever once they got to their destination, a piece of property that he might yet buy. In a strange way it was better this time, ten years after, knowing the happy outcome despite the sad one that inevitably followed.

For what he didn't know on that earlier ride, not yet on that sweet spring afternoon some ten years ago, was Kristen herself. He did not know her in the Biblical sense. They had never yet had full-on sex.

They had not yet seen each other naked. They had not gone beyond flirting and suggestive banter, beyond the occasional kissing and yes, fondling that had taken place intermittently since they were teenagers. In fact, wanting to fuck Kristen predated his entanglement with Sherry. They had partied together well before Carl, then Jim, came along.

"I guess you're right," he replied. "Give me seventy-two whores instead."

Her voice grew impossibly sexy. "How about just one?"

"Sold."

He put the truck in gear, just like ten years earlier, and headed back to Broadway. He turned right amid thinning storefronts, then pure countryside. For old time's sake, he played the game.

"You volunteering for the role?"

"For what role?" she asked, all innocence.

"Like you don't know."

Her crystalline laugh filled the cab. She leaned into him. "Where are we going today?"

"It's a surprise," he replied.

"Okay. Surprise me."

Glancing at his imaginary companion in the passenger seat, he pushed aside thoughts of cancer. They didn't ever talk about her illness, which had disappeared into blessed remission at that point. They never talked about her cancer after it returned. They just didn't.

When they arrived at the cabin on the lake, Kristen's slender body moved with amazing grace as she waded straight into the lake. It was way too cold to go swimming, but she did it anyway.

Exiting the lake, Kristen tore off her T shirt. She tried to get her jeans off next, but couldn't get them past her sneakers. She tripped and fell. Standing onshore with his hands on his hips, Ralph burst into laughter.

Half laughing too, irate as hell, she looked up at him. "Asshole! Help me."

He untied and removed the sneakers, then the jeans. Kristen took off her own bra.

"I've got a scar," she apologized.

"So?" Seeing her skin make his breath speed up.

Ralph took off his jacket and laid it on the ground. He shifted Kristen's hips onto the makeshift bed. He lay down on top of her. She clawed at the top button of his shirt. He helped her undo the rest of them.

She reached for his belt buckle. Ralph looked around. They were all alone, but still.

"Kristen, Honey. You want to go inside the cabin? It's furnished."

She pulled away, a look of astonishment on her face. "You want to break in? I mean my other friends, they do things like that. But you?"

Ralph reddened again. "You think I'm a goody two-shoes."

"I like that about you," she answered, touching his cheek. "You're sweet."

Ralph didn't consider himself especially virtuous, but compared to the crowd Kristen continued to mix with as they separately grew into adults, he was damn law-abiding. In fact, Ralph's only illegal activity was smoking marijuana, which he typically obtained from Kristen.

"We're not going to break and enter, Shithead," he told her. "I have the key to the cabin."

"You do?"

"Of course. The realtor lent it to me. I might buy the place."

Ralph smiled to think that two people who'd just addressed each other as "asshole" and "shithead" could share heart-poundingly awesome sex. They fucked outside first, then again inside the cabin.

When he got to the property on the day of his sixtieth birthday, the former cabin was indeed a burnt-out wreck. He knew there'd been a fire, but still the sight jarred him. No wonder the price had dropped so much.

Upon closer inspection, though, he could see that the stone foundation and chimney remained intact. If he retained just enough of the original structure, maybe the township would let him rebuild on the site. Otherwise, under modern zoning laws, there was no way anybody could put a new building so close to the lake.

He walked the path to the beach, then returned to the truck to get a trash bag. After he cleaned up the cans and broken glass, the sun had begun to drop toward the far shore of the lake. Ralph looked at his watch. He had just enough time to stay and watch the sun set.

Sitting on a rock, he smoked a joint. Moments later he became the rippling water. A gentle breeze rose behind him. Ralph felt acutely alive. Alive and horny. He could have sworn he felt Kristen's hands on his shoulders.

"Go ahead," she whispered.

"I don't know."

"I would do you if I could," she whispered. "You know that."

"I love you," he said back, knowing it was still true.

He thought about the upcoming festivities and wondered for the umpteenth time just what Carl and Jim had in mind. He had no control over the future events. Meanwhile? He took another puff off the joint and put it out.

He closed his eyes and had sex with Kristen. It was amazingly satisfying, all things considered.

Returning to the truck, Ralph felt pleased with the accomplishments of the morning and the just-completed excursion down memory lane. If it were up to him, he'd have declared victory and gone straight home.

Instead, he pulled onto the highway and headed in the direction of Clyde Barnett's farm. He filled up the gas tank at a country store. The plastic-wrapped sandwiches looked appealing, but he decided to hold off.

He followed Jim's directions from memory.

He grew hungrier as it grew darker. Surely, there'd be plenty of food at his sixtieth birthday celebration.

# CHAPTER 5

Katie looked around. The place was humongous. When she looked up, she could discern no actual ceiling, just the naked architecture of rafters and rolled insulation. She found herself alone with Bethany in the cavernous void of a building. The other girls had disappeared to somewhere.

Bethany snapped her fingers twice. "Okay. Give it here."

Judging by the length of the ride, with Katie's knees scrunched over the hump in the back seat, they were about forty miles from Bangor. Forty miles in an unknown direction. Katie regretted not paying more attention to the road signs, though it hadn't mattered since she wasn't driving.

Katie did not have a driver's license yet, because Mom didn't want her to and no way could they afford a second car. She had completed driver's ed at high school, though. She shuddered at the memory of the horrid videos of accidents due to drunk and distracted driving. She shooed away the memory because she, Katie Monahan, had come to this place with all four seniors on the cheerleading squad. Talk about amazing!

"Hand it over," Bethany insisted.

Katie frowned, puzzled. She had nothing to give. She'd left her purse and her polka-dot crocs in Bethany's trunk. Mom's slinky silver heels were affixed to her bare feet. Thanks to practice, practice, practice, she kept her balance on the long, dirt driveway whereas Gina slipped and Tanya actually fell on her butt. Surely Bethany didn't want Katie's high heels. What then?

Katie's stomach lurched. The dress. Bethany wanted her to take off the damn dress again. Way ahead of time.

"N-now? she countered feebly.

"Th-that's right." Bethany mocked Katie's nervous stutter.

"But it's freezing in here." She carefully managed all the consonants, one time each, without repetition.

"Deal with it. Okay?"

What a bitch! Before Katie could wheedle a reprieve, however temporary, Bethany killed that thought.

"The thing is, there's no room to maneuver underneath." She pointed to a skirted table maybe four feet square. "You have to hide until it's time."

"Oh."

The thrill of stripping for a live audience, so vivid hours earlier, had gone mysteriously missing. There was nothing in the whole world Katie hated as much as feeling cold to the bone. Maybe, after graduation, she'd migrate someplace warm like Atlanta. How would she get there? Katie thought about the money.

"When do I get my two hundred bucks?" she challenged.

Bethany laughed before deigning to reply, not the pleasant laugh of a girlfriend but a wicked stepmother's cackle.

"Where would you put it?"

"Good point," Katie had to concede. Her dress had no pockets. She wore no bra or underpants, not even a thong. "About the money?" she persisted. Her voice trembled, but she got the words out anyway. "When do I see it?"

"When you earn it."

Katie swallowed. "After I jump out of the cake, you mean."

"And entertain the guest of honor."

"The birthday boy," said Katie. She added to herself that he was an old fart. She still didn't know his name, first or last. Just as well.

"Yes. Like you said you would."

"But I never ..." Katie's voice trailed off. She didn't know how to finish the sentence. *I beg your pardon, I never promised you a rose garden* played nonsensically in her head.

"What's the matter, Katie?" The question was a challenge, not an escape route.

"Nothing," she muttered.

*Everything*, she thought! The murky terms of the nasty, stupid deal she'd made were beginning to terrify her. She longed to consult Nana, but a private conversation was out of the question with Bethany hovering, a glare on her snobby face, hands on her hips. Earlier in the afternoon, when Katie's nerve started to falter, Nana had appeared.

Nana told her to be brave. Well, Katie would be very brave, brave to the max. Or pretend to be, anyway.

Hell, she could act, no matter what the stupid drama coach said. That would be the senile old bat that Nana had cursed out earlier in the day, the grownup who always skipped over Katie when she handed out the starring roles. Affecting extreme nonchalance, Katie pulled the dress over her head and handed it to Bethany.

"Here you go." Katie's heart sped up, but she refused to let it show. No way!

Bethany stood back and appraised Katie's nakedness, as if Katie's slender perfection was her very own doing. In actuality, Katie's fitness and grace ought to be attributed to Nana. Nana was the one who insisted that Mom sign Katie up for ballet and tap and synchronized swimming lessons. It was Nana who drove her back and forth to class nine times out of ten. Nana always stayed to watch, clapping for every little girl's achievement but loudest of all when Katie's turn came. Mom usually ran errands instead of staying to watch.

"Oh my God. I have the best idea!" Bethany suddenly screeched. Bethany ran from the room, carrying away Katie's dress. Katie hugged herself.

She looked around for some sort of cover, but all she saw were folding chairs in stacks against one wall. A few minutes later Bethany returned, giggling conspiratorially with Gina. The two seniors summarily took hold of Katie's shoulder length hair and coiled it into a tight knot.

"Ouch!" Katie protested.

"Hold still," ordered Bethany.

"It hurts being hot," added Gina. Gina was head cheerleader, the best-looking one too. "And you are very hot, Katie. Figuratively speaking, that is. It's fucking freezing in here."

"I'll say," muttered Katie.

Hearing Gina call her hot made the stinging strands at her temples hurt less. All the cheerleaders were attractive, but Gina with her jet-black hair and dark eyes was truly exceptional. The squad had their own stunt planned for the evening – they kept alluding to it on the drive over. However, nobody had clued Katie in on the details. Nor could she summon the nerve to ask.

"Bethany, hand me that bow."

Gina took a red and white bow, the kind some swanky store might put on a classy gift, and affixed it to the top of Katie's head.

"Now she's the perfect present," declared Bethany.

"Shot time."

Laurel's voice came from behind Katie. She turned to look.

Laurel entered through a doorway Katie hadn't noticed before, followed by Tanya. Laurel carried a tray with plastic shot glasses, a salt shaker, and a cut-up lemon. Tanya held a bottle of tequila. She poured four glasses and handed them out.

"How about Katie?" asked Gina.

"Sure," Katie declared, not sure at all. "Count me in."

"Yes. She needs it." Bethany always had to put in her two cents' worth and be in charge of the whole world.

Katie noticed that all four girls had changed into the tight, cropped letter sweater, plaid miniskirt, and blue-and-yellow sneakers of their uniform. Katie had tried out for cheerleader junior year, making the semifinals before getting cut. By the time tryouts came around again, she already had the job at the Olive Garden.

She hadn't really regretted that turn of events. Cheerleaders had to stand outside in the cold for hours and they didn't get paid. But now, at this moment, she would have given anything to wear the school colors along with the other girls instead of standing buck naked.

"You're a genius!" Bethany clapped her hands in delight as Gina stabbed Katie's bun with a final bobby pin. Gina handed Katie a mirror. For some reason the ribbon-bedecked ball on her head made Katie feel just like a contestant on Toddlers and Tiaras.

"Go on. Get in," ordered Bethany.

Katie thought about throwing a tantrum instead.

Bethany stooped next to the skirted table and pressed a button. Nothing happened.

"Fuck!" she exclaimed. Bethany stood up and hollered, "Jim!"

"Yo!" came from outside the front door.

"Get your ass in here."

Just like that, the brother named Jim stood inches from Katie. He was wearing a plaid shirt and jeans. She stood buck naked except for the sexy shoes that made her even more naked.

"How do you work this asshole thing?" asked Bethany.

To Katie's surprise the same young man who'd ogled her shamelessly hours earlier couldn't even look at her as he demonstrated the mechanics of the cake table. It was ingenious the way one of the panels swung aside. Even better, there was a round trapdoor in the center of the tabletop. It too slid out of the way when you pressed a button. There would be a hole in the center of the cake that Katie was to spring through.

"Very clever," said Katie.

"Thanks. I built it," Jim replied, still without looking at her, let alone in the eye. She liked him better for his bashfulness.

"Yeah, but I thought of it." Carl's gravelly voice sounded.

A blast of cold air poured in from outside as Carl entered the building. Unlike his brother, Carl hadn't turned the least bit shy. He looked Katie up and down and up again, making her blush as he met her eyes with a leering grin.

"Never thought I'd say this. Wish I was the one turning sixty. The one tasting fresh meat."

Katie swallowed. Sixty was way old. Fresh meat, that would be her. She'd get through the night somehow. She wasn't afraid it would hurt. Well, she kind of was, but the pain would be sharp, sudden, and over. Bad shit happened. Shit happened, and you went on. She didn't covet Carl anymore, though, not one bit. She was glad he was not the birthday boy.

As to the old fart? She'd close her eyes and imagine José, who worked as a busboy at the Olive Garden. She would do what must be done, then take the money and run, run, run like the wind. However, Katie Monahan would think really, really hard before she ever agreed to entertain a strange man, to be his perfect birthday present, again. Still, two hundred dollars was a lot of money. A whole weekend's worth of tips.

Voices and male laughter sounded in the distance. The voices grew closer. Katie heard the crunch of gravel on the driveway.

"Get in there!" Bethany hissed.

Nobody had to urge Katie to dive out of sight as a veritable horde of men invaded the room. From underneath the table, Katie heard the clatter of folding chairs. She heard lots of swearing, hoots, and whistles at the sight of the cheerleading squad.

She heard people bring in a couple kegs of beer, the shuffle of chairs being moved into rows. Soon, she gleaned that the men were taking their seats, readying for the coming spectacle.

"Here." It was Gina cracking open the swinging panel. She handed Katie the bottle of tequila, still half full. "Here. Take it."

"I don't know."

"It'll warm you up."

Katie took the bottle and took a swig from it. Paradoxically, she felt goose bumps form on her arms.

"G-gina?"

"You can't chicken out, Katie. It would be understandable if you wanted too, but you just can't. Okay?"

"I know. Bethany would freak."

Gina giggled. "You got that right."

"When do I go on? I want to get this over with."

"Right after us," Gina answered. "We'll sing happy birthday and the birthday boy will blow out the candles. That's your cue."

Katie took another drink from the bottle. Her throat burned. She started to gag.

"Shut up!" came from above.

Even in a whisper she recognized Bethany's authoritarian tone. Katie managed to stop coughing. She turned to thank Gina, but Gina was gone. She took another sip from the bottle, careful not to overdo it this time.

Maybe it was the tequila kicking in. Maybe it was the many warm bodies gathered in the room. Maybe it was her mammalian heat filling the confined cube under the table. In any event, Katie was no longer the least bit cold. She felt warm and relaxed, that is, so long as she didn't dwell on the mess she'd gotten herself into. Oh well. She would do whatever it took to get to the other side of the evening. Whatever it took.

Outside her cube cacophony reined. *Cacophony*. She liked the sound of the word. Though she rarely went to games, especially now that she worked evenings at the Olive Garden, Katie knew the sequence of cheerleading routines by heart. She also knew that the watching men were getting drunker by the minute.

Apparently, the girls wore no panties under their short, short skirts. Katie wished she could watch Gina do cartwheels, but she couldn't. Katie took another swig off the bottle, this time not worrying about covering her coughing. Things were way too wild and raucous and out of hand for anyone to hear her. But wait! There were footsteps approaching her table. She called it her table since it was built for the occasion by the better brother named Jim.

Somebody started to sing. Others joined in, mostly way off-key. *Happy birthday to you. Happy birthday to you.* Oh, now she understood! They were carrying the birthday cake to the table. The thing had to be huge to work as planned, a huge ring with a false center. *Happy birthday, dear Ralph*. So the guy having a birthday's name was Ralph. What a goofy name, she thought.

Katie tipped back the bottle one last time. She was surprised to discover just a sip left. Apparently she'd chugged quite a few times while the cheerleaders jiggled through their chants. Good thing she'd thought through the logistics beforehand.

Bethany was absolutely right that there was no room to maneuver under this table. The covered hole above her was just big enough for a slender girl to carefully slip through.

She hoped they had set the cake into position just right.

*Happy birthday to you.*

Katie crouched beneath the opening. She pressed the button, and the cover slid aside, just as Jim had demonstrated. Fortunately, the cake was in perfect position.

Katie held her arms tight against her sides. It was time to play the role of a sex goddess. No, it was time to morph into the sex goddess. Why stop there? She would become the goddess of love. And passion. As Nana always said, if something's worth doing, it's worth doing right.

"Make a wish, Dad," she heard Jim say.

Everyone congratulated Ralph because, old fart though he surely was, the birthday boy had managed to extinguish all sixty candles in one breath.

She stood up, wriggling smartly through the center opening. Without disturbing a crumb, Katie lifted her arms above her head. Surrounded by trailing wisps of smoke, Katie proudly tossed her head. Except her hair didn't swing in response. She remembered the silly bow on top of her head. That struck her as hilarious.

She raised the empty tequila bottle like Lady Liberty's torch.

Katie laughed wildly while all the men applauded.

## CHAPTER 6

"Cool," said Ralph. That felt utterly insufficient for the occasion, so he added the word "Amazing."

Carl stepped up, wielding an unfamiliar tool above his head in every direction. "How do you work a fucking electric knife?" he asked.

"I'll show you." One of the cheerleaders, not the prettiest one on the squad, approached the table. "Try plugging it in first, Asshole. There must be an outlet someplace in this dump."

"Wait a sec, Bethany." Jim appeared next carrying a normal kitchen knife.

The smiling girl who had emerged from the center of the cake was very pretty. She was also awfully young and entirely naked. She didn't look like a stripper or a slut. She looked, more than anything, like jailbait.

Now what, Ralph wondered. What the fuck?

"She's all yours, Dad," said Carl. Carl had a smirk on his face.

Jim looked away.

"Is that right?" Ralph shook his head. "Listen, boys. I loved the show. But," his voice trailed off. It was hard to explain why he did not want to walk off with this achingly pretty, apparently willing creature. Truth be told, he was way hungrier than horny after the very long day.

"Thanks, but no thanks," he said aloud, his voice firm with finality.

He saw tears form in the girl's eyes.

"No, honey. Don't take it like that. Please."

Carl whispered something in his ear. He thought he heard right, but he asked just to be sure. "What?"

"I said she's a virgin."

Everybody heard. Cake girl gasped.

"Well, you are, aren't you?" prodded Bethany.

Ralph had an urge to smack that bitch. Something in the voice of Bethany reminded him of Sherry.

Cake girl got a wild look in her eyes and didn't reply. For a second Ralph thought she was going to faint.

Ralph turned to Carl. "Where are the other seventy-one?"

"Huh? What the fuck?"

The black-haired cheerleader, the really good-looking one that Ralph truly found enticing, laughed and put a hand on Carl's arm. She got the joke.

"He means like the suicide bomber at the gates of heaven. He wants seventy-two virgins, not just one."

"That's right," said Ralph. He had made a lame joke in very bad taste. Too late - he stuck with it to get past the awkward moment he was supposed to passionately appreciate. "I want all seventy-two virgins or none at all."

He turned to Cake girl. "Go get dressed, Honey. Nice job jumping out of the cake."

Ralph started toward the front door. He didn't give a damn if it was his birthday party. There was nothing to eat at his birthday party except one bowl of broken pretzels and the goddamn cake. Oh, and an abundance of beer, which clashed disgustingly with cake. More importantly, he had no intention of spending one second alone in the company of an underage girl. She did look like jailbait. Scared out of her wits, too.

Suddenly Carl was blocking his path. "What the fuck, Dad? "We went through all this trouble and spent a lot of money."

"It's my party, and I'll fly if I want to," answered Ralph.

"Good one, Dad." Jim was there too, by the front door, trying to defuse the situation.

Carl's tone got downright nasty. "So you think it's funny, Bro?"

"Take it easy," said Ralph.

"Easy," mocked Carl. "I'll tell you what's easy. That hot girl. If you don't want her, I do."

"Hey, what about me?" protested Jim. "I put up half the money for tonight."

"Go ahead, flip a coin," said Ralph. "Me? I'm out of here."

But there were people he liked in the room, friends he hadn't seen in years or maybe even decades. So it took him a while to get his coat and make his way toward the front door.

Meanwhile, he was dimly aware that George Hoskins flipped a quarter and that Jim called "heads" and lost.

"All yours, Bro."

Jim was always a fair sport, a gracious loser. He heard Cake Girl burst into tears.

Carl did a war whoop. "Come on, Katie."

Ralph's blood froze. He turned toward Cake Girl, who truly looked terrified now. Carl had a proprietary arm around her, his hand dangling over her left breast.

"Katie," repeated Ralph. "What's your last name?"

"M-Monahan," she stammered.

"Deal's off, Carl."

"You can't do that," whined Ralph's always difficult, older son.

Ralph hated confrontations, especially ones involving family. He told himself to let it slide. Let the story play out. What was this foolish girl, this Katie Monahan, to him? She was not his responsibility. There was no connection between the two of them. None. A flash of

Kristen on the lakeshore, hands on her hips above low-riding jeans, appeared. Disappeared.

Ralph heard his own firm voice repeat, "I said the deal is off," with solid conviction.

By now the whole room was attune to the crisis. Everyone stopped to gawk. Carl was way too drunk to hold his tongue.

"Fuck you, Dad."

"Easy, Bro," said Jim.

"Fuck you too!" shouted Carl.

Still holding the electric knife, Carl swung at Jim, who ducked like a professional boxer and neatly evaded the blow. Carl staggered and almost fell. The crowd laughed. Utterly irate, Carl lunged toward the nearest toothy grin, which happened to belong to one of the cheerleaders.

Carl lifted the knife. The cheerleader screamed like a movie star. Ralph seriously doubted if, at sixty, he was still stronger than either of his sons. But he leapt into action anyway, stepping between Carl and the panicked cheerleader, shoving Carl against the wall and pinning him there. Ralph's fingers dug into Carl's flailing wrists.

Yup, Dad was still stronger. Plenty stronger.

"Drop it," Ralph ordered.

Carl stopped resisting and dropped the knife.

"Now apologize," ordered Ralph.

"Jesus, Dad. To that twat?"

"To me."

"Why the hell should I?"

"Because I'm not just your father."

"Oh yeah?"

"That's right. I'm also your boss."

Carl tried to hide it, but Ralph saw him flinch. He felt the fight go out of his son. Ralph loosened his grip, and Carl's hands dropped harmlessly to his sides. The roomful of sloshed partygoers waited for the magic words to flow: *I'm sorry, Dad.* What would that fit old fart do if they didn't come?

Everybody waited for Carl's apology.

In his peripheral vision, Ralph saw Katie Monahan hugging herself, tears streaming down her cheeks, melting her makeup. The hot, dark cheerleader, the one he would not have turned down, walked into the frame carrying a silver dress. She handed it to Katie.

"God, Gina. Thanks."

Gina. So that was her name. Ralph filed the detail in his brain. He could still do that, keeping compartmentalized life straight. He didn't have to look up dimensions on projects. Even that burnt-out cottage he'd driven to hours earlier, he remembered the layout exactly. The names of all the kids in his first-grade picture? Not so much.

Not long ago he'd hauled out a box of photos and gotten a rude shock. Mr. Flawless Memory could name only four of twenty-four scrubbed second graders, the little girls all in dresses. Some of the boys wore jackets and ties, but Ralph wore a plaid shirt that could have come from today's closet.

Katie's smeary face disappeared, and the girl's hips wiggled with impatience as she forced the stretchy neck over the oversize bow atop her head. Some of the honey-blond hair, the same color as Kristen's used to be, came loose. Watching the slinky dress unfurl over flawless shoulders, breasts, belly button, bush, thighs, Ralph's focus shifted along with the rest of the room. The crowd forgot all about Carl and a missed apology.

Ralph's wound-up adrenaline slowly abated. Even as he watched the pretty girl, ancient arguments with Sherry sprang to mind. She had nagged him often about Carl's sullen insolence, through the years together and then the ones apart. *You got to talk to that boy and teach him shit from shinola.* Ralph had tried, but the lesson never stuck.

Ralph meant to repeat the command, "Apologize!" But the word literally stuck in his throat. A strangled animal grunt sounded instead. Jim shot him a concerned look, concerned but oddly animated too. Ralph could tell that Jim wanted Carl's comeuppance to play out in public.

Nope! It was not meant to be. The hell with humiliating his own kid in front of the madding crowd. Something told Ralph that, from now on, Carl would be considerably easier to manage at work.

Jim handed him some money.

"Here. We owe her this much. Okay?"

Ralph put the bills in his wallet without counting the money. Next, he turned to the girl in the silver sheath.

"Come on, Katie," Ralph said. "Let's you and me fly out of here."

## CHAPTER 7

The tight gray sheath protecting her breasts, hips, and thighs felt like salvation itself. Katie headed toward the old guy, the birthday boy. Ralph was standing near the open barn door. The pointy toe of Mom's left shoe snagged on a busted pretzel. Katie stumbled. "What's the matter with me?" she puzzled.

Inside her boiling brain, Nana laughed out loud. "You're drunk, Sister."

Nana had never ever called Katie "Sister" before. Katie liked the sound of it, the equal status. Grown-up status. The ballet training Nana had long ago decreed kicked in, and Katie did not fall.

Party time swelled and churned in every direction. She made her way toward Ralph, swaying and smiling at the odd challenge of staying upright. She thought about greedy, grabby Carl being so stubborn and stupid. Carl was behind her somewhere, too close for comfort. She tried to speed up. What a bad sport, refusing to cave when he had obviously lost. Any way you sliced the cake, old Dad came out the winner.

Katie belonged to the winner. Why did it take ages to cross the last ten feet of floorboard to reach The Man?

Ralph stepped forward, clearing the yawning distance in one stride. He put his arm around her. She leaned into him. Umm. Somebody started up the music. Hard rock.

"Who wants to dance?" yelled Bethany at cheerleader volume. "Come on, Jim."

Chairs got shoved aside as those two began to shimmy and shake. Others joined them. Katie saw Carl pull Gina onto the dance floor.

Meanwhile, Ralph led her outside where the cool breeze felt heaven-sent. Stars spangled the night sky. The shrill chorus of peepers competed with the pulsing bass of the speakers. The frogs gradually prevailed as the mismatched couple made its way between a double row of vehicles. Trucks and bikes and cars lined the gravel road for what seemed like forever. So Ralph had a whole lot of friends. He was popular enough to make Katie jealous.

Katie jumped at the sudden digital beep. Just ahead a set of headlights blinked twice in reply. She called herself stupid.

"So there you are." Ralph chuckled. He turned to Katie. "I was starting to wonder where my pickup went. Pickup truck, that is. Not that anybody'd steal my wheels. They'd nab your friend's Lexus."

"Bethany's not my friend," answered Katie with vehemence. But Ralph had a point – his pickup looked old and plain. Clean though.

"No, probably not," she told Ralph.

He opened the passenger door. "Go on. Get in."

"Okay."

She took the high step into the cab of Ralph's pickup, acutely conscious that she still wore no underwear. Unlike Carl, Ralph did not take advantage of the opportunity to grab Katie's butt. Nor did he run around the truck and gawk as she displayed her gash.

Instead, he stooped and picked up somebody else's beer can. He got behind the wheel and started the truck.

Soon they were on a smooth paved road, humming along at a crisp pace. Now what did the evening have in store? Sure, Ralph had carried her away from danger like some gallant knight. But maybe he wanted her for himself. Was she expected to give the birthday boy a blow job? Let him fuck her? Fucking was fast, and it didn't really hurt. Not that much, so she'd heard.

So if it was up to her, she knew which lewd act she'd choose. She had a pack of condoms in her purse, but shit! Her purse was in Bethany's trunk. She sure as hell didn't want to get pregnant at age eighteen. Would she have to swallow to make the other act complete?

Katie felt her stomach churn.

"Mind if I open the window?" she asked, not waiting for an answer. But she couldn't find the right button. Oh God, what if she threw up in the front seat of his truck, his neat and clean truck? The window magically slid down as he pushed a button on the driver's side.

"Thanks." She drew several breaths of spring air.

"No problem."

Where was he taking her? She didn't dare ask. As she looked in the mental rearview mirror, she thought how the crowded barn stank of spilt beer. She never wanted to see the world's biggest super bitch, Bethany, ever again. Screw every one of those stuck-up cheerleader sluts. And they were sluts, too, doing split jumps in cropped sweaters without their bras on, flipping cartwheels without any panties. Sluts every bit as much as Katie herself. So there.

She tried to catch a numbered road sign to gauge her whereabouts, but there weren't any. The truck was moving too fast to let her read the names of occasional cross streets.

Oh well, she trusted Ralph completely. Whoa. Trusted him to what? Well, to be gentle. Not to hurt her. Not to brag about whatever they might eventually do tonight. He might be old, way old, but the man was still decent looking. Salt and pepper hair was kind of cool. The liver spots on the hands? Katie ordered herself not to go there. No, it would be best to find out what he wanted and get it over with. Collect the two hundred bucks.

*Go directly to jail. Do not pass go. Do not collect two hundred dollars.* What was the monopoly board doing in her brain at a time like this?

She slid a tentative hand across the gear shift and onto Ralph's thigh. Katie's heart began to pound.

"Don't!" snapped Ralph.

Katie pulled her hand away. She leaned out the window and took several deep breaths. Relief washed over her. But was she really out of the woods? As if to mock her mental question, they entered a stretch of deep, dark woods. Maybe he had some nasty fantasy planned, starring Katie Monahan.

Suppose he had a video camera set up in a grungy motel room. So that's where they were headed, a cheap motel. She willed away the flutter in her stomach. She sneaked a glance at Ralph. His hands gripped the wheel so hard she wondered if there'd be dents left behind.

She gave him an inquiring look.

"Just don't touch me," he muttered between clenched teeth.

"Why not?"

For some reason, Ralph turned beet red in the face and struggled against strong emotion. "Because she, I mean you, my former fiancée ... because Kristen would step right out of her grave and strangle me. I guess they didn't literally bury her; they cremated her. Or so they tell me. I wasn't there."

*No*, thought Katie. *Mom wouldn't let you come.*

But that didn't make any sense. That didn't compute. Who was the man at the wheel?

Struggling for control, Ralph went on. "I guess she'd have to congeal out of dust and ashes to come back after me, but she would do it. She'd find a fucking way. The Kristen I knew would chop my balls off if I ever, ever touched one hair on her precious granddaughter's head."

Before he could finish the thought, Katie interrupted. "You knew my Nana?" Kristen was Nana's actual name.

"You bet I did."

"Wow." It was all she could think to say.

"She'd be ashamed of you, Katie."

"She would not!" Katie shot back. Then she reddened. But I am, she thought to herself. I'm ashamed.

To her surprise, instead of lecturing more, which she probably deserved, Ralph laughed. "You're right. Kristen didn't judge."

Exactly! Nana never lectured; she never blamed. Somehow Ralph knew that.

"She loved spectacles. And sex." He looked away. "I shouldn't have said that last bit."

The dawning realization shattered Katie's world. "You're the one she was in love with."

"Yeah."

"When she died."

"Bingo."

"Wow. My mom hates you."

"Still, huh?"

Katie giggled in spite of the serious turn of the conversation. "Mom is like that. She's the grudge queen."

"Well, in this case I can't say as I blame her."

Little shards floated in and out of focus in Katie's brain. Nana did once have a boyfriend named Ralph. How could Katie have forgotten? She vaguely remembered a medium-sized man with dark hair and, according to Mom, beady eyes. Katie glanced at the driver. His eyes were maybe a little small. Ralph had bought a rambling, rundown house. Nana wanted to live there after it got fixed up. Katie had gone to a party there once upon a time. Was it a birthday party? Yes, another birthday party, talk about weird! Miss Russell, the senior litt teacher, would call it ironic.

Whose birthday?

She closed her eyes and thought as hard as she could. She remembered a big turquoise swimming pool. She saw a chocolate cake with sixteen burning candles. Nana was laughing and pushing Ralph to help some older boy blow them all out. But they wouldn't go out because they were trick candles. Nana's trick candles. Katie could still taste the chocolate frosting, the cold vanilla kiss of ice cream in a plastic spoon.

Mom had gotten screaming mad at Nana afterward. Why was that? Because Katie wasn't supposed to go to Ralph's house, not ever for one single second.

"Why does my Mom hate you?" asked Katie. "What did you do?"

"I broke Kristen's heart."

Ralph's sigh held all the regret in the universe. Katie watched him fight for control. Oh God, what if he started crying? That would be unbearable, worse than handing her dress off to Bethany earlier in the increasingly outrageous night.

Ralph got his shit together. He didn't cry - disaster averted.

Suddenly she had a slew of burning questions for Nana's last boyfriend, the man Nana loved and Mom hated. For instance, who was the boy turning sixteen? Katie had no brothers or sisters, not even a first cousin. None of that had mattered when she was little because she had Nana. The two of them even dressed alike sometimes. Nana said that dressing alike made Nana and Katie twins. Mom snorted and said that was really stupid.

Ralph's next question surprised her. "You want to get something to eat?" The contents of her stomach shifted. The threat of throwing up was still very much with her.

"Okay," she replied anyway.

"Good. Because I'm starving. You think they'd have food at a party."

You would think that. But no, there had been no table full of food at the party.

"What are you in the mood for?" asked Ralph.

"You choose," she replied. "Anyplace but The Olive Garden."

## CHAPTER 8

Ralph refused to accept that, with Katie Monahan in tow, he had managed to get good and lost. He went back over the first three turns in his head. He was following Jim's memorized directions to Clyde Barnett's farm in reverse. Normally he could do that kind of thing, no problem. But he rarely drove to unfamiliar places in the dark. At night the world did not look the same.

Both new company trucks, shiny black with his company logo, were equipped with GPS. Carl and Jim drove the new trucks home every night. *What's up with that?* Ralph berated him.

He kept a Maine atlas behind the passenger seat. There was something unformed about the young woman in said passenger seat. She evoked more than she resembled Kristen. Unlike her grandmother, who could easily drink him under the table, Katie was looking green about the gills. He didn't dare ask her to lean forward so he could get at the damn atlas.

Instead, he made the situation into a challenge. His excellent sense of direction asserted that they were heading due east. Sooner or later, they would cross I-95. He gave himself twenty minutes, until half past midnight, to bisect the interstate. The gas tank was half full, plus he kept a spare five gallons in the truck bed under the cap. He was pretty sure the plan would work so long as the country road stayed straight and true.

They rode on in silence. He was acutely aware of Katie's presence, of the two-generation gap. He switched the high beams off for an approaching vehicle, then back on. As the clock struck twelve thirty, he pondered whether his cell phone was functional this far out in the woods. He didn't want to spook Katie by finding out that it didn't work. Mercifully, the girl said nothing, though he could practically hear Kristen's voice declare, "Admit it, Dude. You're fucking lost."

When they finally saw a sign for I-95, the dashboard clock read 12:50. With relief Ralph met the Lincoln exit. He turned onto the southbound ramp and accelerated onto the empty interstate. The speedometer quickly topped seventy. He set cruise control at seventy-five.

"Hope the cops are someplace else," he said.

Katie smiled weakly. "Me too."

Ralph's stomach rumbled. Now that he knew where the fuck he was, hunger returned to the forefront in spades. He didn't care whether Katie wanted to stop or not. He made a beeline for the 24-7 truck stop just north of Old Town.

Twenty minutes later they pulled into the parking lot. Ralph hadn't been to the restaurant in years, but he knew the complex well. They bought diesel for the trucks and gas for the chainsaws when they opened and closed some thirty seasonal cabins in the vicinity each spring and fall.

Opening and shutting down cabins was a Jim job. Jim's jobs required one hardworking, responsible guy, unsupervised, from start to finish. You handed them off, and you deposited the check. Carl, on the other hand, was always bringing "issues" - what a loaded word - to Ralph's attention. Still, Carl was the better foreman on big jobs. Carl enjoyed ensuring that others followed his instructions to the letter. Carl liked the power that came with hiring and firing workers. He never missed a day of work.

So there was a place for both sons in the business. But it was Jim's company he greatly preferred. Guilt stabbed. Maybe Kristen had been lucky having just one daughter. And one granddaughter.

As always, a bevy of semis occupied the huge, dirt parking lot across from the truck stop, their diesel engines idling because it was cheaper than shutting them off and on. He explained this to Katie as they pulled to a stop in the paved area reserved for cars and pickups. Nobody worried about thieves.

“I hear the prices went up and the portions went down,” he said, “but the food’s still excellent according to Jim.”

“I got to puke,” announced Katie the instant her feet hit pavement. And she did.

“Are you okay?” he asked afterward.

“Uh huh,” she lied gamely. “I think so.”

“Well, thanks for not doing that in my truck.”

He started toward the back door of the 24-7 Truck Stop. She followed, then stopped short in the glaring light over the back door.

“Oh great, just great!” she lamented.

“What’s the matter now?” asked Ralph.

“My new dress!”

For the second time that night, he watched Katie’s eyes fill with tears, reminding him of the helpless child he’d last seen sitting on a hospital bed. Ten years ago.

“It’s pretty bad,” he acknowledged. The form-fitting silver fabric was liberally streaked with vomit.

"Go in by yourself, Ralph. I’ll wait in the ... you don’t want me in your truck either. Do you?”

“Not really.”

“What should I do?” she wailed.

He sighed. “Wait here."

Ralph strode toward the building without replying. He hoped that the travel store wouldn't fail him. He found the entrance to the travel store locked.

"Fuck!"

"Hey man. Over here."

Ralph turned. He recognized the night manager at the fuel desk. How many years could a man spend in one dead-end job?

"Hi Donny. What's with the store?"

"Closes at midnight now."

"No shit."

"I can let you in, though."

"I don't want to get you in trouble," Ralph began.

"You won't." Donny reached under the counter for a keychain. "For special customers. Gordo's idea."

Gordo was the youngest of the four brothers who owned the 24-7, the goofy-looking kid that got no respect from the rest of the family. From what Ralph could see, Gordo had more of a brain for business than the other three siblings put together.

Ralph followed Donny into the travel store. Women's fashion was not the 24-7's strong suit. He found some hideous, shocking pink sweats that might fit Katie. That or day glow orange. He wandered to the men's section and settled instead on a plaid shirt, men's small, and a pair of jeans in the size that Sherry used to buy.

Donny rang in the order. "Charge it to the company account?"

He was about to say a reflexive yes, then thought better of it. You own a business for thirty years, you learn what not to memorialize in the company records.

"Nope. It's personal," Ralph replied. He spied the rolled towels behind the cash register. "How much is a shower these days?"

"Five bucks."

"Five bucks!" Ralph shot back.

"Yeah, I know. Forget it, right?"

"Add it in. It's for a friend. Is anybody in the shower room now?"

"Nope."

"Keep it that way for a while. Okay?"

"Female friend, I take it."

Ralph nodded. Donny's questioning look craved details, but Ralph had no desire to explain the night's events. He handed over his personal credit card, feeling a mild rush of virtue for not cheating the government, and signed the slip.

He brought Katie in through the back door and pointed toward the shower room and handed her the rolled-up towel.

"Here. Take this. This too."

She looked inside the plastic bag. "Wow. Thanks."

"You're welcome. Go get cleaned up."

"Okay."

"Meet me in the restaurant. I'm fucking starving."

As she walked away, the plastic bag swung in time with her hips. No trace of vomit marred the back of the stripper's dress. The fabric was as form fitting as silver paint. Ralph gave himself permission. He imagined lifting the dress and bending her over from behind. He felt Kristen's ghostly breath in a sudden gust of wind and shuddered.

Katie reached the doorway. She turned and waved. He quickly looked away. Katie disappeared. Ralph strode toward the front entrance into the restaurant.

"Sit anywhere," said the sign. Except for the crowded truckers' table, the place was practically empty.

Only after sitting down in the third booth on the west wall did it hit him. He'd sat at that very table with Kristen and another couple named Jim and Amy many years earlier. They were friends of Kristen. Like most of Kristen's friends, Ralph no longer associated with them. In fact, he actively avoided her friends. He marveled that, after ten years, guilt lurked that close to the surface.

"All by your lonesome?" asked the waitress. She wasn't young, but she wasn't bad either. The white uniform that buttoned down the front fit rather snugly. She reached for the other place setting to remove it from the table.

"No," he replied. "I'm with my granddaughter." The lie came so easily that it didn't feel like one. "She's in the ladies' room."

"Something to drink?"

"Coffee. Black."

"What about her?"

Ralph felt himself blush. He should know what his granddaughter liked to drink, but except for chugging tequila, he didn't have a clue. The waitress stood, pencil poised. Kristen used to drink diet ginger ale – with or without a dose of gin.

"Got any diet ginger ale?" he asked doubtfully.

"We have diet 7Up."

"Is that close?"

"Very."

"That then. With plenty of ice cubes," he improvised, remembering how Kristen had liked her drinks.

"I'll be right back with your drinks. Specials are on the board."

Ralph read through the specials, all distantly familiar, all more expensive than they used to be. He already knew what he wanted. He always ordered fried clams at the

24/7. He pretended to look at the menu, all the while mentally panicking about the upcoming conversation. It was necessary, damn it, to explain himself to this charming and bewildering child-woman.

Why? Because he was responsible for her isolation. Not totally, not like the missing father, whoever the hell he might be, but in part. He had behaved badly. He did not rise to the mighty occasion. Kristen had constructed a princely hero of him, but the vision wasn't real.

In point of fact, when the engagement ended, it was Kristen who had severed the tie, screaming, "Get out, get out, get out!" Surely, that was an overreaction. All he had said was that he needed to slow down the train. Did that make him a worm?

Back then, *Till death do us part* felt like the icy breath of oncoming winter once Kristen's cancer resurged. Instead of bracing for the void alongside his fragile fiancée, he had literally cried on Sherry's shoulder. That intimacy led upstairs to the bedroom, after which, much as he still loved Kristen, nothing could ever be the same.

Face buried in the menu, he remembered the logic of his position. Kristen was dying of cancer. Lung cancer. She already lacked half a lung after a prior surgery. This time the tumors were small and widespread. Surgery wasn't an option. Radiation would start immediately, with chemotherapy to follow.

Soon there'd be no more smoking dope and screwing under the stars. No more poking each other, dozing on the couch, to stay up for Saturday Night Live. Ralph and Kristen strove to be the first beings on earth to get the latest George W. joke.

Instead of the most fun he'd ever had with anyone, he'd be driving a basket case to and from doctor appointments. He imagined her thick, honey-blond tresses falling out of her head as he grabbed hold. It was one of their naughty secrets, that she loved the taste of danger when he pulled her hair during foreplay.

Why should he put himself through months and months of accelerating hell when the outcome couldn't be changed? What was more, Kristen's daughter Alice was dead set against the marriage. Especially once they gave Kristen a maximum of a year to live. Didn't Kristen want to spend the little time she had left with her only daughter and her only grandchild? That would be Katie, who was taking a very long time in the 24/7 bathroom.

He imagined the ancient argument replaying between Kristen and Alice.

"How could you take up with that man and abandon your family? asked Alice.

"I don't want to be alone anymore," replied Kristen.

"You're hardly alone. You have us."

"But I'm in love with Ralph. We used to be just friends, but now we're so much more. I always wanted to be with him – you know that. He's rehabbing a whole house for me."

"The place is a wreck," Alice would have countered.

"He'll fix it." That would be Kristen.

"It can't possibly get done in time."

"Screw you! I'm not gone yet."

"No, not yet."

"That was mean, Alice."

"I'm sorry, Mom. But what about Katie?"

"She can come visit me at Ralph's house. She can spend the night anytime she wants."

"No, she can't. I don't trust him. He has beady eyes."

"He does not."

"I don't want Katie going over there. Ever. Period. End of story."

Might Kristen have lasted longer if they'd become man and wife? Over her daughter's vociferous objections, Kristen had chosen Ralph. And then he bailed. He convinced himself that it would be stupid to marry Kristen, though he surely loved her. The stark reality was that he lacked the courage to wed a person who was near death.

As if by black magic, all the joy drained out of the woman he adored. Just like that, she lost her sassy edge. The decline in Kristen's health following the breakup was downright precipitous.

From the couple glimpses he later got from the hospital hallway, Kristen suffered a most unkind death. He came to say goodbye. But he didn't dare enter, not with Alice in the room. What if he'd known the cruel power of a broken promise? Maybe then he would have mustered the wherewithal, somehow, to meet her at the end of the aisle. How odd that Kristen, not one bit religious, had wanted a church wedding.

And even if they didn't ultimately marry, there still might have been a way to stay together if only he had not already slept with Sherry. Confess his sin or hide it from the love of his life? Either way, he had stained their joining beyond repair. It still made him feel like a worm.

"Ready to order?" The waitress's voice interrupted Ralph's mental second guessing.

He recovered quickly. "I'll have the fried clam basket. She'll ... I don't know. She got sick earlier. As a matter of fact, I'm starting to worry."

'What's her name?" asked the waitress.

"Huh?" asked Ralph, thinking that the answer might be Kristen.

"Your granddaughter. I'll go check on her."

"Katie. Her name is Katie."

"I'll be right back."

She smiled, a lovely expression undiminished by the lines crisscrossing her cheeks. For the second time on this very late night, Ralph felt a surge of desire as he watched a woman's ass approach the door to the shower bay. He wondered about the waitress's name, then her age. More than fifty, he figured. Less than sixty.

The old lyric that he'd misquoted back at Clyde Barnett's farm played in his head. *It's my party, and I'll cry if I want to.* Leslie Gore used to sing that song. That name would mean nothing to Katie or her entourage including the enticingly hot cheerleader named Gina. Gina was way too young for him and he knew it. He allowed himself a moment of birthday self-pity.

The intriguing waitress at the 24-7 was another story. Still, she too was surely younger than Ralph.

Shit. Wasn't everybody?

## CHAPTER 9

Katie stood in front of the bathroom sink in the ladies' room with her sleeves rolled up. New flannel felt cozy against clean skin. The new jeans fit perfectly. The sneakers were too big, but she appreciated the extra room because her toes ached after getting scrunched into points. Who knew chunky old Mom had such narrow feet? Katie pressed the soap dispenser and scrubbed vigorously. Bit by bit the streaks of vomit disappeared from the silver stripper dress.

Katie heard the outside door open. There was a separate men's shower room, but both facilities stood at opposite corners of a long hallway. The corridor had been well lit but deserted, she recalled. Fear gripped her. Then, miraculously, a woman's voice called her very own name.

"Over here," Katie answered as her pulse slowed toward normal.

A blonde lady in a waitress dress walked in. She wasn't young, but she had a good figure.

"You okay?" the stranger asked.

"Yeah. I'm getting some puke off this dress."

"Oh. That kind of sick."

"Huh?" Katie asked.

"He said you weren't feeling well."

"Who did?"

"Your grandfather. Who do you think?"

Katie started to protest. Then she realized how awful the truth would sound. *Actually, I jumped naked out of his birthday cake in a barn full of strange men. Why? For two hundred dollars so I could buy blingy jeans just like Bethany's. Who's Bethany? The meanest, snotty bitch on the planet.*

Instead, Katie said, "Yeah. He bought me new clothes. He's really nice." It occurred to Katie that those coveted two-hundred-dollar jeans wouldn't look or fit one bit better than the pair she had on.

"What should I tell him?" asked the waitress.

"Tell him I'll be right out."

"You want to order?"

"Now? I don't suppose you brought a menu."

"No. But we got everything. Including breakfast."

"What's he having?"

"Fried clam plate."

"Me too."

Katie never ordered seafood, but this was a night like no other. As the waitress walked away, Katie called, "And a diet ginger ale with plenty of ice."

She wrung out the stripper dress and rolled it into a log. She put the dress on top of Mom's shoes in the plastic bag from the travel store. With luck she could get the dress into her dresser drawer and the shoes back in Mom's closet without getting interrogated. Fifteen minutes earlier she'd have sworn she'd never eat again, but she found herself insanely hungry. What would they talk about at the table, though? It was so hard to talk to boys, let alone to an old man she barely knew.

Whenever Katie dated a new boy, Mom always repeated the same piece of stupid advice: Identify the common interests you both share. Well, she and Ralph had Nana in common. They had Nana and the earlier events of the evening - stripping, puking, getting lost, and refusing, just like a man, to admit it. They'd best stick with Nana for small talk. Nana was Kristen to him. She said the name to the empty ladies' room.

Katie didn't know anybody else named Kristen, so Nana owned the name. Ralph had gotten close to Kristen, maybe even closer than Katie. Definitely closer in a certain way. Katie's mouth curved into a smile as a string of images unrolled.

She remembered exactly how Nana looked naked, from the curved scar below her shoulder blade to the surprisingly perky tits. Unlike Mom, Nana didn't hide her body when they changed at the swimming pool. Nana gawked shamelessly at all the women in the changing shack. She made nasty comments afterward that were so funny that even Mom couldn't help but giggle.

Mom. Suddenly Katie knew exactly what she and Ralph could talk about. Would talk about. Had to talk about. Maybe Ralph even had the magic answer. She headed to the restaurant feeling more determined than ever in her life. She would find a way to bring up the subject. She would not lose her nerve.

As sometimes happens, the path simply appeared.

"Feeling better, Katie?" asked the cheerful blond waitress as she set down two identical dishes of coleslaw.

"Sure am," she replied. "I'm starving."

"Thanks for checking on her," Ralph put in.

"So. Which side of the family are you on? Mom or Dad?"

Katie observed the man on the other side of the table fight a look of surprise. Before Ralph could invent an answer, a loud "Hey Loretta!" came from the truckers' section.

` "Sorry. I got to deal with that bunch."

The waitress named Loretta hastened away.

With the word "Dad" still hanging in the air, Katie posed the question. "Ralph, do you know who my father was?"

"No, Honey. I don't."

Katie's sunny mood deflated. The stammer she hated reared its ugly head, like always, at the worst possible time. "I j-just thought y-you might." She swallowed a surging lump. "You know. Know something."

"Did you ask Alice?"

"Of course," Katie answered. "Lots of times. Not lately though. I mean, all she ever said was that she met him in Boston, and that he was in the Navy. One time she said his name was Bill, but she might have made that part up."

He sighed. "Yup. That was about all Kristen ever got too." Ralph picked up his fork. He put it down. "Here's what I do know. Kristen tried to find your father. Your grandmother tried really hard."

"When?" asked Katie excitedly.

"Right after you were born." Ralph swallowed. "She asked me to come with her. We weren't together then, we were just old friends. She was scared to go there alone with good reason. So, I drove Kristen to Boston."

"And?"

"Jesus, Katie. I don't know if I should be the one telling you this shit."

"You have to. You have to!"

For once Katie's voice projected into the entire dining room. Loretta looked their way. Even the truckers at the long table turned.

"Hey, calm down.," Ralph pleaded.

"Only if you tell me every single thing you do know."

"Okay. But don't tell your mother where you heard it. If you think she hates me now, well, this just might make it worse."

"I won't say a word to her. I swear."

Ralph talked while Katie absorbed the astounding truth. She already knew some of the circumstances, enough to conclude that Ralph's information was utterly reliable. She knew that Mom had been engaged, briefly, to a medical student. She knew that Mom dropped out of nursing school when the future doctor dumped her, and that she lived in Boston for a while.

"Your mom worked in a bar. Kristen got the name of the place off of one of Alice's pay stubs. Then we discovered it was in the Combat Zone."

"What's that?"

Ralph shook his head. "It seems quaint now in a weird way. You had to seek out the pornography back then. It was limited to a few really scary city blocks, barely a stone's throw from the four-star hotels."

Katie had never been to Boston.

"Did you find Bill?"

"Yes and no."

"What do you mean, 'yes and no'?"

"We found Bill all right. And Jim. And Fred. And Tom, Dick, and Harry too."

"I don't get it."

"Do I have to spell it out?"

"Yes," said Katie, though she was starting to get the picture.

"Alice waited tables. She never touched a drop until last call. Then she'd join a table full of sleaze balls, gulp down five in a row, and leave with whoever wasn't too wasted to get it up. Sometimes there'd be more than one. She was a real party girl, your mom."

"No way!"

"Back then she was."

Katie was utterly stunned. Mom was so responsible. Mom was such a prude.

The odor of fried clams rose from a plate right in front of Katie. She hadn't even noticed when Loretta set it down.

"I don't get it. Why in the world would she morph into a whore?"

Ralph shrugged. "People do strange things on the rebound. Hell, I remarried my ex-wife. Talk about stupid."

"Not as stupid as my mom," retorted Katie. "I mean, wasn't there, like, rampant AIDS around that time?"

"Yup. And it was a death sentence back then."

"Wow."

"AIDS, herpes, and the clap. Not to mention the crabs, which are damn near impossible to get out of the house. Not that I'm speaking from personal experience, of course."

Katie giggled, unsure whether he was kidding or confessing.

Ralph went on. "As to STD's, so far as I know, Alice got away unscathed. Except for getting pregnant with you, that is."

"Nana, I mean Kristen, must have crucified Mom. The having-fun part might have been okay, but not using birth control? Sheesh!" Katie wondered if she should refer to Mom as Alice, but that was too enormous a leap.

"Kristen had a temper all right. Don't I know it! But when it came to what took place in Boston, she was just plain sad."

"You mean for me," Katie said the realization aloud. "Because I'll never meet my father."

"Sad for you. Sad for Alice. Even for Bill or Fred, or whatever his name was, who will never get to know his lovely daughter."

"Thanks, said Katie. "Thanks for the compliment."

"Kristen never told your mother about that journey she and I took to Boston, playing detective, unfortunately without solving the case. Maybe Kristen and Alice talked about important stuff near the end. Somehow, I don't think so."

Katie didn't think so either. The tension between Nana and Mom had never abated.

"Look. Here's my take. Alice left town because she had pride. She couldn't stand being an object of pity. I wouldn't like that either, I know that much."

This made sense to Katie, Mom wanting to melt into a giant metropolis where nobody knew her name, where nobody ever, ever talked about her humiliation.

Ralph went on. "But then, when Alice found out she was pregnant, she came back home anyway. She quit drinking. She straightened out on a dime. All because of you."

Katie absorbed this new perspective.

"I still don't get why Mom went wild. I'm sure it was embarrassing for her to lose the guy who became a doctor. But still."

Ralph smiled. He had lovely even teeth. She could imagine Nana wanting to kiss him.

He said, "And I don't get why a smart girl like you would take her clothes off at an old man's birthday party."

Katie blushed deeply. "Can we, like, never talk about that ever again?"

"It's a deal."

For the first time Ralph dug into his plate of food. Katie did the same. The food tasted salty, greasy, and delicious.

"Hey Ralph. How come you've got way more fries than I do?" she exclaimed.

It was true. He did have twice as many fries. "I don't know."

Katie turned and glanced toward the kitchen. The blond waitress stood by the door with her arms folded. She was staring right at their table.

"Do you know what I think?"

"What?"

"I think Loretta likes you."

Ralph looked toward the kitchen. As if she'd been caught in the act, Loretta turned away.

"You want some dessert?" he asked.

Katie didn't want the meal to end, so she said yes.

"Me too."

"You know what?" asked Katie. "If I tell Loretta it's your birthday, I'll bet you anything she gives you a free piece of cake."

"Don't you dare!" answered Ralph.

"Why not?"

"Because I'll have to say the word sixty. That'll make it real."

"Good point," conceded Katie.

"Besides which, I want a piece of apple crumb pie with whipped cream."

"Make that two." Following his lead had worked out so far.

While they waited for Loretta to take their empty plates, Ralph asked Katie what she planned to do after high school. She mumbled something, but he pressed for a real answer. That led to how much she loved to dance, especially when she felt the music.

Maybe she didn't mind so much being in the chorus because she got to be part of the spectacle without the pressure. The idea was a new thought, and its truth filled her to the core.

She told him how she'd love to dance in a big musical on Broadway, maybe just once, because she wanted to have a house and a family too, not just perform onstage all the time.

"No family without a husband, though," she finished. "That's too hard. Way too hard."

"I told you you're a smart girl."

"Thanks. Meantime, they offered me a full-time job as a hostess at the Olive Garden. You think I should take it?"

"Is it more money?"

"A lot. But no tips. So, I'm not sure. I think I'd like it, though, being up front, wearing a pretty dress instead of a dorky uniform. It's not exactly the path to Broadway. I could live at home and save up, though."

"There are Olive Gardens everywhere. Including New York City. They all run on the same business model, I surmise."

That was likely to be true too. Katie hadn't thought of that.

Loretta showed up with the dessert menu, but Ralph said they didn't need menus.

"Two apple crumb pies with whipped cream."

"You got it."

After dessert, Loretta promptly brought the check. "You pay up front at the register."

Ralph, in a plaid shirt and jeans, stood up. Katie wiped her mouth with her napkin and rose as well. She followed him toward the cash register.

"What's this?" Ralph stared at the check. Right next to the total he found a seven-digit phone number surrounded by hearts.

"Hey you two," called their waitress. "You look like twins."

It struck them both at the same time - they were indeed dressed alike. The squares in Katie's red-and-black tartan were maybe a hair smaller. But the faded jeans might have come from the same rack. Katie and Ralph roared with laughter. They were both still cracking up out of control when they hit the parking lot.

"Hey!" called Loretta after them.

Their waitress stood by the open front door of the restaurant.

“What’s so funny? Inquiring minds want to know!”

## CHAPTER 10

Ralph steered the truck toward the curb, carefully gliding alongside it before pulling to a stop.

"It's the brown duplex up ahead," Katie told him.

"I know where you live," he replied.

"You do?"

She sounded astonished. That made him sad. He made light of the moment instead.

"Sure. I had to steer clear of Alice."

She rewarded him with that engaging giggle. Kristen's laugh had been bolder, bawdier. Kristen's laugh lingered longer, too, he reflected, as seriousness of purpose reclaimed the moment.

"Look, Katie," he said. "There's something I need to say to you. It's important."

"But I'll never ever, in my whole entire life, pull a stupid stunt like – "

He cut her off. "It's got nothing to do with tonight. It's about, well, about ten years ago. I should have married Kristen. I wish I did. I'm sorry."

He took a deep breath, fighting the mounting surge of regret. Tears even threatened. "I always knew in my heart it was the right thing to do, but my brain said no.

Logic said *Don't marry a dead woman walking*. Think of the medical bills. Skip the suffering, man. There is no happy ending here. You know?"

"That kind of makes sense," Katie offered.

"All the sense in the world," Ralph agreed. "Besides which, your mom hated my guts. Alice didn't trust me."

How much should he tell his companion poised on the doorstep of adulthood? The part about sleeping with Sherry while he was engaged to Kristen, that guilt he did not need to share. But the other guilt he did need to spill. His future depended on it.

"Here's what I didn't fully understand, not until this moment," he began.

Ralph closed his eyes and thought back. He stood in the hallway of the floor called "palliative care." Kristen was hooked to a gigantic, whooshing oxygen tank. Alice sat nearby in a chair, her nose buried in a magazine. About eight years old, Katie sat cross-legged on Kristen's bed, holding her grandmother's frail, shaky hand. He described the scene as best he could to Katie. Amazingly, she remembered the moment.

"That should have been me," he affirmed. "I should have been the one holding her hand."

"But I wanted to be there," Katie protested.

"No. I should have put my foot down. I should have stepped in."

"Nana needed me."

"It wasn't right! A deathbed is no place for a child." He thought of Katie's unflinching bravery in the face of unspeakable tragedy. "It was my place. Mine."

"Oh."

"And maybe," Ralph continued, the insights coming fast and furious, "just maybe you'd have some real friends now instead of that mean bitch who talked you into throwing away your innocence tonight. I'm not telling you to save yourself for your wedding night. That's up to you. But don't do like you did tonight."

"Almost did," Katie amended the narrative. "Only you stopped me."

Ralph hesitated anew, then persisted with his inquiry, softening his tone as best he could. "It's true that you don't have a lot of friends. Right?"

"No," said Katie. "I don't have real friends. Probably I shouldn't admit this, but -" and then she stopped.

"What, Honey?" asked Ralph.

He watched her take a deep breath. "I still talk to her. Nana, I mean. Sometimes. Maybe a lot. Does that make me crazy?"

He shrugged.

"Thanks a lot!"

Ralph sighed. "If I could go back and marry Kristen, I would. You always hear people say that, if they had to do things all over again, faced with the same circumstances, they'd do the exact same thing. Not me."

"No," said Katie. "That's like admitting you never learned anything in your entire life."

"Exactly. And oh-so-proud of staying stupid," added Ralph.

They shared a good laugh over that. They rode in silence for a minute. It felt comfortable being quiet together, as it had with Kristen.

Finally, Katie spoke. "So, you do think I'm crazy talking to a dead person."

Ralph smiled. "Then I'm crazy too. I spent time with Kristen this very afternoon."

"You did?" Katie sounded pleased.

"I did," He affirmed.

He thought back to the lakeside property, the time spent there long ago and the memory savored.

Ralph said, "It would be really cool to get a complete do-over. Let's do it. Let's play pretend like little kids."

"Sure. I'll bite," answered Katie. Her face grew animated and dreamy. "What was the wedding like for you and Kristen?"

It was still hard for her to say her grandmother's first name, he could tell. He smiled.

"Don't you remember? You were the flower girl."

"Oh yeah. Of course I was. The wedding was outdoors, wasn't it?"

"Beside a lake," he improvised.

"And then. Did she get better afterward?" Katie asked hopefully.

"No, Honey. I couldn't make that happen. But she did live two whole years instead of only eleven months. They were good times, even when Kristen started sleeping a lot. I fixed her a place in the living room when she couldn't come upstairs anymore."

"Is there a fireplace?"

"Yes."

"I remember that. I used to come to your house after school sometimes. The bus would drop me off there instead of at daycare."

"You helped me scrape down the walls upstairs. I was still renovating the house then."

"I couldn't have been much help at eight years old."

"Don't sell yourself short. Besides, you were damn good company."

"Sometimes you helped me do my math homework."

"Yes, I did."

"Mom's good at math. Nana wasn't."

Ralph kept improvising, inventing a better past. It might have turned out that way, had he done what still felt like the right thing to do. It would have been tough, but he could have shared Kristen's courageous waning days, and come out a better man on the other side.

He plunged ahead. "You stayed weekends with us too. Alice even stopped hating me after a while. She saw how happy Kristen was. Plus, Alice suddenly had time for a life of her own. That made a difference."

"Did my mom get married too?

"I don't know, Katie. You tell me."

"No," said Katie. "But she made real friends too. Mom and her new friends did girls' night out once a week."

In real life, Mom didn't have any more true friends than Katie did.

"The important thing," Ralph continued, feeling suddenly inspired, "is that I became your grandfather when I married Kristen. We stayed in touch afterward, you and me, after she passed. In fact, I still am your grandfather. That part can be true. It is true. From now on I am your grandfather."

"What does that even mean?" asked Katie, looking both hopeful and frightened.

"It means I've always got your back," he answered without hesitation. "Any time you're in trouble. Anytime you need some advice. Somebody to talk to for no reason at all. Okay?"

"I like that."

"Let's say you're someplace you don't feel safe and you need a ride home. Call me. Anytime. Day or night." He reached into his wallet. He noticed the two hundred-dollar bills. He pulled out a business card and handed it to Katie. "My cell-phone number is on there too. That's my personal number. Call me anytime."

She took the card and stuck it in her shirt pocket.

"Middle of the night. No questions asked. Right?"

"I don't know about that. It depends on what kind of trouble you get yourself in."

She looked crestfallen.

"Hey, I'm a grownup. And your grandfather. And a very old fart."

"You are not."

"Am too."

This time she did not protest. "You wouldn't tell my mom though, right?"

"That I can promise."

Ralph put the idling old truck in gear and pulled into Katie's driveway. "Guess this is it," he said. What a mundane sentence, given all the ground they had covered. He tried again. "Thanks for one unforgettable birthday."

"Are you going to call Loretta and ask her out?"

"I might," he allowed, knowing that he would.

Katie leaned over, gave him a quick hug, and reached for the door handle.

"Hey, you forgot something." Ralph reached into his wallet and held out the two crisp one-hundred-dollar bills.

"I don't deserve the money," she protested. "I didn't, you know, deliver."

Ralph put the two crisp bills into her hand and gently folded her fingers closed.

"Then give them to someone who does."

"Okay," Katie agreed, and just like that they parted ways.

Katie spoke the words aloud, to give them power, as she mounted the steps to the front porch. "Be asleep, Mom. Be asleep. Please be asleep."

Good, she saw no lights on in their half a house. She still didn't have her purse, just the plastic bag from the travel store. In the dim glow of the porch light, Katie bent and quickly found the extra key under the mat. As if moving backstage during a live scene, she entered without emitting a single stray sound.

"Katie, is that you?" Mom's voice came from the kitchen.

Shit!

Katie tried to sneak upstairs, but Mom walked into the living room before she could get away. The interrogation began.

"Katie, you're late."

"But I told you we might go out after I got off work." Had she? Probably not, but Mom wouldn't know for sure either.

"Who dropped you off?"

"Some friends of Bethany's. Their father, actually."

That was the absolute truth. Sort of.

"Where's your uniform?"

Katie indicated the plastic bag in her hand. "I puked on my dress." Still the literal truth, if not the whole truth.

Mom put her hands on her hips.

"Were you drinking?"

"Yes."

She waited for Mom to go ballistic, but the honest answer had thrown her mother off guard. To Katie's amazement, the next thing Mom did was smile.

"Well. It's not necessarily a bad thing. I bet getting sick taught you a lesson."

"I learned my lesson tonight all right," Katie heartily agreed. She started toward the stairs.

"Are those the jeans you wanted?"

"Uh huh."

That was an outright falsehood, except that Katie now treasured the travel-store jeans way more than that pricey pair with the fancy logo on the butt.

"Well, they fit." Mom shook her head ruefully. "Wish I had an ass like that."

Katie giggled. "Thanks."

"How were the tips tonight?"

Suddenly Katie knew exactly what to do next. "Good, but I'm not going to be a waitress anymore."

"You're not?"

"No. I'm going to take that hostess job. Not forever, but for now. For one thing, it's a promotion. Plus, Olive Garden is a big company."

Like her newly-minted grandfather said, she could transfer to anywhere in the country, maybe the whole wide world. Plus, she finally had something to put under "Future Plans" in the program that would get handed out to everyone on graduation day.

Katie continued speaking without forethought, saying, "I want to keep living here so I can save up some money."

Mom said, "Of course you can live here. You are welcome to stay here for as long as you wish."

"I'll pay rent though. Two hundred dollars a month. Starting now."

Katie plunked Ralph's money, the money she did not deserve, onto the coffee table. Before Mom could react or ask any more tough questions, Katie scampered up the flight of stairs.

Quietly, carefully, she entered Mom's room and replaced the silver high heels in the closet. Just in case, to cover her tracks, she flushed the toilet in the upstairs bathroom. Breathing a sigh of relief, she reentered the hallway.

"Katie?"

Mom's voice came from the bottom of the stairs. The hallway light came on.

Katie kept heading for the sanctuary of her own space. Suddenly she spotted Nana blocking the doorway to Katie's bedroom.

"Answer your mother!" commanded Nana, shaking her finger at Katie like she'd never done in real life.

Reluctantly, Katie turned around. She stood in the light at the top of the stairs.

"What, Mom?"

"You're my angel."

Nana smiled, blew them both a kiss, and vanished.

www.ingramcontent.com/pod-product-compliance
Lightning Source LLC
LaVergne TN
LVHW011030110826
845149LV00015B/3363

* 9 7 9 8 9 9 5 3 5 0 3 0 9 *